KB100411

과도기

아시아에서는《바이링궐 에디션 한국 대표 소설》을 기획하여 한국의 우수한 문학을 주제별로 엄선해 국내외 독자들에게 소개합니다. 이 기획은 국내외 우수한 번역가들이 참여하여 원작의 품격을 최대한 살렸습니다. 문학을 통해 아시아의 정체성과 가치를 살피는 데 주력해 온 아시아는 한국인의 삶을 넓고 깊게 이해하는데 이 기획이 기여하기를 기대합니다.

Asia Publishers presents some of the very best modern Korean literature to readers worldwide through its new Korean literature series 〈Bilingual Edition Modern Korean Literature〉. We are proud and happy to offer it in the most authoritative translation by renowned translators of Korean literature. We hope that this series helps to build solid bridges between citizens of the world and Koreans through a rich in-depth understanding of Korea.

바이링궐 에디션 한국 대표 소설 089

Bi-lingual Edition Modern Korean Literature 089

Transition

한설야
과도기

Han Seol-ya

ASIA
PUBLISHERS

Contents

과도기

Transition

1

창선이는 사 년 만에 옛 땅으로 돌아왔다. 돌아왔다니
보다 몰려왔다. 되놈의 등쌀에 간도에서도 살 수 없게
된 때에 한낱 광명과 같이 생각되어지고 두덮어놓고 발
끝이 향하여진 곳은 예 살던 이 땅이었다.

그러나 두만강 얼음을 타고 이 땅에 밟아 들어보아도
저기서 생각던 바와는 아주 딴판이다—밭 하루갈이 논
두어 마지기 살 돈만 벌었으면 흥타령을 부르며 고향으
로 가겠는데—이렇게 생각던 터인데 막상 돌아와 보니

1

Chang-seon returned to his homeland after four years. Or, rather, he was driven back. When he found himself unable to live even in Jiandao because of the harassment of the Chinks, the only seemingly bright spot that he was still instinctively drawn to was his homelands.

But, when he finally treaded across the frozen Duman River and back home, everything seemed to betray the expectation he'd been cherishing for so long in foreign lands. He thought if only he had money enough to buy a plot of land worth one day

자기를 반겨 맞는 곳이라고는 없었다. '고국산천이 그립다. 죽어도 돌아가 보리라' 하던 생각은 점점 엷어졌다. 그리고 옛 마을 뒷고개에 올라선 때에는 두근두근한 새로운 생각까지 났다.—무슨 낯으로 가족들과 동리 사람을 대할까! 개똥밭 하루갈이 살 밑천이 없지—

"후—"

길게 숨을 돋우었다. 그래도 가슴은 막막할 뿐이다. 그는 하염없이 턱 서며 꾸동쳐 지었던 가장집물[1])을 내려놓았다. 한숨 쉬어가지고 좀 가뿐한 걸음으로 반가운 고향을 찾을 차렸다.

"여보, 그 어린애 좀 내려놓고 한숨 들여가우."

"잠이 들었는데…… 새끼두 또 오줌을 쌌구나. 에그, 척척해."

아낙은 '달마'같이 보고지[2)를 한 어린것을 등에서 내려놓았다. 오줌에 젖은 그의 등에서는 김이 뉘엿뉘엿 일어났다.

"여보! 이거 영 딴판이 됐구려!"

그는 흘깃 아낙을 보며 눈이 둥그레졌다. 고향은 알아볼 수가 없게 변하였다. 변하였다니보다 없어진 듯했

of plowing, and a rice paddy good enough to plant several *mal* of seed, he could return home easily, humming the "Heung Ballad" all the way back. However, on his journey back, nowhere seemed welcoming to him anymore. The thought: "I miss my homeland, its mountains and rivers—I'll come back even if I end up dying there" became weaker and weaker along the way. When he finally reached the pass behind his old village, even a new anxious thought began to nag at him: How can I face my family and villagers when I return? I don't have capital to even buy a rotten field worth one day of plowing...

"Whew!"

He breathed a long sigh. Still, he felt desolate. He stood and started to take down some packed household goods from his back. He decided that he needed a brief rest in order to return to his beloved home village on lighter steps.

"Honey, put the baby down and let's have a rest," he said to his wife.

"It's sleeping. Hm, it went again," she drew in a small breath of disappointment. "It's wet."

Their baby was wrapped like "Dharma" and she took him down. A small column of steam was ris-

다. 그리고 우중충한 벽돌집 쇠집 굴뚝—들이 잠뿍[3] 들어섰다.

"저게 무슨 기계간인가?"

"참 원, 저 거먼 게 다 뭐유? ……아, 저쪽이 창리(그들이 살던 곳)가 아니우?"

아낙은 설마 그래도 고향이 통째로 이사를 갔거나 영장이 되었으리라고는 믿지 않았다. 어디든지 그 근방에 남아 있을 것 같았고 아물아물 뵈는 것 같기도 했다.

"저— 바닷가까지 기계간이 나갔는데, 원 어디가 있다구 그래……가만있자 저기가 형제바위(바닷가에 있는 두 바위)고 저기가 쿵쿵(파도가 심한 여울)인데……."

"글쎄…… 저게 다 뭔가."

아낙도 자세 보니 참말 마을이라고는 보이지 않았다.

"최 면장네랑 박 순검네도 다— 어디 갔는지!"

"그런 사람이야 국록[4]을 먹는데 어디 간들 못 살라구."

"그래도 우리처럼 훌훌 옮기겠소. 삼백 년인지 오백 년인지…… 어느 임금 적부터라던가……."

겨울 해는 벌써 서산머리에 나불거린다. 검은 바다에

ing from his wife's back, which was wet with the child's urine.

"Goodness! Our home village has changed completely!" he said to his wife, wide-eyed.

His home village had changed so completely it seemed unrecognizable. Rather than having changed, the village seemed to have simply disappeared. The place was crowded with chimney after chimney, projecting out from dreary-looking brick and steel buildings.

"Is that some sort of a machine workshop?" he wondered out loud.

"Oh, my, what on earth could those black things be? ...Oh, is this really where Chang-ri, our home village, used to be?" his wife seemed in disbelief. Had the entire village had moved or disappeared? Wherever it might be, the village surely was somewhere nearby, she supposed. She felt she could see it somewhere, though she wasn't certain.

"There... the machine workshop stretches out to the beach over there. So, where on earth do you see our village?" He then added, "Let's see, that's the Brother Rocks over there, and that's the Rapids over there..."

"Well... What are they all, then?" Upon careful ob-

서 불어오는 짜디짠 바람이 살을 에는 눈기운을 머금고 획획 분다. 그들은 걸을 힘이 나지 않았다. 간도 땅에서 한낱 태산같이 믿고 온 고향이요 구주와 같이 믿고 온 형의 집이 죄다 간곳없으니 어디를 가면 좋을지 알 수가 없게 되었다.

"그래도 가봅시다. 저기 가서 물어보면 알겠지."

아낙은 아직도 무엇을 믿기만 하는 모양이다. 가보면 무슨 도리가 혹 있을 것 같았던 것이다.

"원, 땅과 물어본담, 바다와 물어본담."

창선은 다시 짐을 걸머지었다.

"점심밥이 좀 남았던가?"

"웬 게 남아요…… 줄 게 없는 밥이 암만 먹어야 배가 일어서야지."

그들은 턱도 없는 곳으로 향하여 걸어갔다. 길쭉길쭉한 벽돌집(관사)이 왜병대같이 규칙 있게 산비탈에 나란히 섰다. 평바닥에는 고래 같은 커다란 공장들이 있다. 높다란 굴뚝이 거만스럽게 우뚝우뚝 버티고 있다. 이쪽에는 잘방게(蟹) 같은 큰 돌막이 벽돌집 서슬에 불려갈 듯이 황송히 짜그리고[5] 있다. 호떡집에서는 가는

14

servation, his wife could not find their village at all.

"Village Chief Choi's house and Police Officer Pak's house—where could they be?"

"They live on government salaries. They would do fine wherever they go."

"Still, could they move as easily as us? Heard they've been living here for three or five hundred years...from the time of the king whatchama-call-it."

The winter sun was already flickering near the western hill. From the dark sea the salty wind was gusting harshly, carrying the smell of flesh-lancing snow. The couple didn't feel like walking. They didn't know where to go. Their home village they'd believed to be as reliable as Mount Tae, and they'd considered their savior when they had left Jiandao, had disappeared into thin air together with his house.

"Let's go anyway. If we ask around, I'm sure we can find out where they've all gone to," the wife said, still hopeful. It seemed she believed they could find out what to do by just going.

"So, will we ask the land or the sea?"

Chang-seon loaded his luggage upon his back again and asked her, "Any leftovers from lunch?"

연기가 난다.

검퍼런 공장복에다 진흙빛 감발[6]을 친 청인인지 조선사람인지 일인인지 모를 눈에 서투른 사람이 바쁘게 쏘다닌다. 허리를 질근질근 동여맨 소매 기다란 청인들이 왈왈거리며 지나간다. 조선사람이라고 보이는 것은 어울리지 않는 감발을 이고 상투를 갓 자르고 남도 사투리를 쓰는 패뿐이다. 옛날같이 상투 찌고 곰방대를 든 친구들을 하나도 볼 수가 없었다.

창선은 그런 패를 만날 때마다 무엇을 물어볼 듯이 머뭇머뭇하곤 하였다. 그러나 웬일인지 말이 나가지 않았다. 그리하여 여러 패를 그저 지나 보내었다. 입에서 금시 말이 나갈 듯하다가는 혹 예 보던 사람이 있겠지 하며 딴 데를 휘휘 살펴보았다.

얼마 가다가 그는 저 멀리서 흰 옷 입은 사람이 하나 오는 것을 보았다. 역시 멀리서 보아도 예 보던 사람같이 흙 냄새 고기 냄새 나는 텁텁한 사람이 아니다. 그러나 혼자서 오는 것이 어떻게 정이 들어 보였다.

"원, 모두 험상궂은 사람들뿐이지…… 사람조차 변했는지…… 공연히 나왔지. 이거 어디 살겠소."

"What leftovers...? No matter how much of that useless rice we eat, our stomachs won't stand up on it, will they?"

They walked on towards the strange new town. A row of long brick houses—dormitory buildings— stood in line atop the slope like Japanese military troops. Across the level land, there were large factory buildings—as large as whales. Tall chimneys rose out of each one stout, and arrogant.

Across the street, a large hut crouched humbly like a crab, almost as if it were afraid of being blown away by the fierce glare of the brick houses. A thin stream of smoke arose from a Chinese pancake house.

Hurrying this way and that, and wearing navy blue uniforms and mud-colored headbands, were streams of unfamiliar-looking people. Their nationalities were unclear—whether they were Chinese, Korean, or Japanese, neither the husband nor wife could be sure. Chinese-looking men wearing long sleeves and tightly tied wastes passed by, chattering loudly. The only Koreans visible were those without their topknots. They wore unbecoming headbands and were speaking in Southern dialects. No one had worn a topknot and carried a

아낙은 근심스러운 푸념을 한다. 와보면 무슨 수가 있을 것 같은 생각이 많이 덜어졌다.

"저―기 오는 사람과 물어보면 알겠지. 설마 산 사람 입에 거미줄이 쓸라구…… 노동이라도 해 먹지 뭘."

창선은 인제 막다른 골목에 서는 듯한 생각이 났다.

"여보―"

그는 문득 앞에 오는 흰 옷 입은 사람을 부르며 주춤하였다.

"여기 저― 바닷가 창리가 어디로 갔는지 모르겠소?"

"창리요?"

그는 창선이의 내외를 아래위를 훑어보며 대수롭지 않게 대답을 한다.

"저 고개 너머 구룡리로 갔죠. 벌써 언제라구―"

"구룡리요?"

창선은 숨이 나왔다. 구룡리는 잘 아는 곳이다. 고향은 아니나 사촌 고향쯤은 되는 곳이다. 집이 몇이 있고 길이 어떻게 난 것까지 머리에 남아 있다.

"저 구룡리 말이지요. 그래 창리 집들은 죄다 그리로 갔나요? 혹 창룡(그의 형) 씨라고 모르겠소."

long pipe like that in the past.

Whenever Chang-seon passed by those strange people, he was hesitant. Although he wanted to ask them questions about who they were and what was this place, for some reason he could not force himself to do so. Accordingly, he let many groups of those people pass him by. Although the words were on the tip of his tongue, he just looked away in search of old acquaintances.

After walking and observing in this way for a while longer, he saw someone in white clothes coming in his direction. Even from a distance, he could see that this man, too, was not humble folk reeking of soil and fish like his old neighbors. Still, he was walking alone and so he somehow came across as friendlier.

"My—all the people look so frightening here... even the people might have changed... This wasn't a good idea to come back. How can we live in a place like this?" Chang-seon's wife murmured anxiously. She was no longer sure if they could discern what to do here.

"I suppose we'll have some idea after we ask that man coming towards us. As long as we're alive, I don't think spider webs'll hang from our mouths...

"그걸 누가 아오."

흰 옷 입은 노동자는 공연히 서슬이 나서 지나간다. 창선은 그 사람 가는 편을 흘깃 바라보고는 아낙을 향하여 애오라지 웃음을 보였다.

"구룡리로 갔다는구려. 원, 웬 판국인지 이놈의 조화를 누가 안담."

"그 ×들 해필 창리라야 맛인가……."

"거기가 알장이거든. 너르고……."

두 내외는 바로 구룡리 뒷재를 향하여 걸어갔다. 좀 기운이 나는 듯했다. 짐을 진 남편의 등판도 좀 가뿐해진 것 같고 아낙의 보퉁이도 얼만큼 가벼워지는 듯했다.

2

구룡리 뒷재는 끊어졌다. 철도길이 살대같이 해변으로 내달았다. '후미기리[7]'에 올라서니 '레일'이 남북으로 한없이 늘어져 있다. 어디서 왔는지 어디까지 갔는지 끝 간 데가 아물아물 사라진다. 놀랍고 야단스러워 보였다. 그러나 그만치 눈에 서툴고 인정모가 보이지 않

At worst, I can work as a day laborer." Chang-seon felt as if he were standing at a precipice.

"Hello!" Chang-seon hailed the man and hesitated before proceeding with "I wonder where Chang-ri... over there at the beach has gone?"

"Chang-ri?" The man looked up and down at the couple and casually answered, "It moved to Guryong-ri over there, beyond that pass. It's been quite a while..."

"Guryong-ri?" Chang-seon had a sigh of relief.

Chang-seon knew Guryong-ri well. Guryong-ri was not his home, but it could probably be called his cousin village. He still remembered how many houses there had been and how roads in that village had laid.

"Oh, that Guryong-ri! So, did all Chang-ri villagers move there? Do you by any chance know Chang-ryong, my brother?"

"How should I know?" The man in white clothes seemed upset for no reason at all and marched away. Chang-seon watched him go and then turned around and forced a smile at his wife.

"Looks like they moved to Guryong-ri. What the heck? Who knows what on earth is going on here anymore?"

왔다. 소수레나 고깃배가 얼마나 정답게 생각되는지 몰랐다. '풍…… 왕— 왕—' 하는 기차 소리는 귀에 야츠러웠다.[8]

그는 꿈인 듯 옛일이 새로워졌다. 산비탈 고개 남석 다방솔[9] 그늘 아래 낮잠 자는 그 옛일이 새로워졌다. 두세 오리 전선줄에 강남 제비 쉬고 가는 그 봄철에 밭 갈던 기억이 그리워졌다. 구운 가자미(물고기)에 참조 점심[10]을 꿋꿋이 먹고 엉금엉금 김매던 그 밭이 정다워 보였다.

동리 아이들, 처녀 총각—검둥이 센둥이 앞방네 뒷방네가 첫 새벽부터 수소 암소들 척척 거넘겨 타고 '아리랑' 노래를 부르며 소 먹이러 다니던 것도 이 근방이다.

"개똥네야, 소 먹이러 가자."

이렇게 부르면,

"쩡냥(뒷간)이냐. 그래라, 나간다. 쌍돌이 헛간쇠 안 왔니."

이렇게 대답하며 소를 몰고 나선다.

"야, 네 소는 양지머리가 감추었구나."(살이 찌면 양지머리가 불쑥하게 된다)

"Those x, why did it have to be our Chang-ri...?"

"Chang-ri's the best location, you know. It's spacious..."

The couple walked straight towards the pass behind Guryong-ri. They felt a little encouraged. The burden on the husband's back felt lighter, and the bundles on the wife's back felt somewhat lighter, too.

2

The hill pass behind Guryong-ri was cut down the middle. Railway tracks ran briskly through it like an arrow. From the crosswalk, they could see the rail stretch endlessly north and south. Both the place from which it came and the place to which it was headed receded into haziness. It was truly grand and impressive. But, it looked as unfamiliar and unfriendly as it looked amazing and impressive. In comparison, an oxcart or a fishing-boat felt so much more caring to them. The sound from trains like "chuchu... wowowow..." didn't feel pleasant to their ears.

"우리 소야 숫소니까 그렇지."

"야, 숫소는 암내[獸慾]를 내서 봄이면 여빈단다."[11]

이렇게 얘기들 하는 사이에 소 먹이는 아이들은 네다섯…… 십여 명씩 모인다. 그러면 아리랑타령이 나온다.

꿀보다 더 단 건 진고개 사탕

놀기나 좋기는 세벌상투(총각이 머리채로 짠 상투)

아리랑 아리랑 아라리요

아리랑 고개로 날 넘겨라

시냇가 강변에 돌도 많고

이내 시집에 말도 많다

노래와 얘기로 해 가는 줄을 모른다. 때때로 소를 말뚝에 매어 놓고 수수께끼, 서울목돈(돌 유희), 사또놀음, 소경놀음, 각시놀음, 말놀음도 한다. 그러다가 겨울이 되면 바닷가에 나가서 고기그물에 고드름같이 줄 달린

As if they were dreams, Chang-seon was re-minded of old days. He remembered napping in the shadow of the young, thick pine trees on the slope. He missed spring days when he'd plowed fields while swallows rested on the electric lines on their way to Jiangnan. He imagined the fields lov-ingly, the fields he'd weed, crouching after a lovely lunch of fried flounder and millet.

It was around this area where the village children, women, and men—Geomdung-yi, Sendung-yi, Apbangne, and Duitbangne—all rode their oxen and cows to graze, singing the Song of Arirang.

When a friend called, "Gaeddongne, let's take the cows to graze!" Gaeddongne would emerge, driv-ing his cow and answering, "Oh, Jjeongnyang! Al-right, I'm coming. Hasn't Ssangdori brought his cow from the shed yet?"

When a child said, "Hey, where's your ox's bris-ket? It's hidden!" someone would respond, "That's because it's an ox."

"Yes, I hear oxen usually gets thinner in spring because of the mating season."

Chattering like this, the children would gather one after another, driving their oxen and cows, and

고기도 뜯는다. 이 고장은 대개 절반 농사로 절반은 고기잡이 때문에 어린아이들도 두 가지 일을 하는 것이다. 고기 잘 잡히는 해면 어린아이들도 하루 수삼십 전벌이를 한다. 그 때문에 처녀 총각이 만나는 도수가 많고 또 예사로 얘기들을 한다.

이러한 중에서 창선이도 지금의 아낙을 맞들였던 것이다. 시쳇말로 하면 연애를 하였던 것이다.

"야, 이거 안 먹겠니. 뉘—?"

창선은 개눈깔사탕을 사가지고 와서는 소를 먹이다가 일부러 순남이(그의 아낙) 곁에 가까이 가서 개눈깔사탕을 쥔 손을 번쩍 들며 "뉘—?" 하고 소리를 친다.

"내—"

"내다."

아이들은 연방 이렇게 나도 나도 소리소리 외친다.

"옛다, 순남이 첫째다."

창선은 누가 먼저 "내—" 했겠든지 그건 아잘 것 없이[12] 애초의 예산대로 한두 알 순남이에게 주고는 남은 것은 제 입에 모두 쓸어 넣는다.

"야 순남아, 씹어 먹지 말고 녹여라. 누가 더 오래 녹

eventually forming a group of four or five to ten or more. Then came the Song of Arirang.

Sweeter than honey is the Jingogae candy
Fun to play with is a braided topknot (topknot for unmarried man)

Arirang arirang arariyo
Please send me over the Arirang Pass

There are lots of rocks on the riverbank
There are lots of talks in my in-law's house

They'd sing and chatter, and they wouldn't know when the sun would set. Sometimes, after tying their charges to stakes, they'd tell riddles, play the Seoul fund game (rock game), the magistrate game, the blind man game, the bride game, and the horse game. In the winter, they went to the beach and helped take down the frozen fish that hung from the net like icicles. As adults did both farming and fishing in this area, children contributed to both in these ways. On years with good fish harvests, the children sometimes earned twenty or thirty *jeon* a day. And of course, the boys and girls would spend

이나 내기할까."

그러면 여러 아이들은 부러워서 침을 꿀꿀 넘긴다.

"저 간나새끼 사(私)를 쓴다. 내가 먼저다."

"옳다, 저 애가 먼저다. 그담에 낸데…… 니 무슨……
순남이 네 각시냐."

"내 순남이 에미와 이르지 않는가 봐라."

이렇게 철없는 불평이 터진다. 그러면 멋모르는 순남
이는 신이 나서 악을 쓴다.

"야 이 종간나새끼, 각시란 기 무시기냐…… 야 이 간
나야, 너는 울 어머니와 무스거 이르겠니. 너는 언제 쌍
돌이 꽈리를 가졌니."

"이 간나, 내 언제 가졌니."

이렇게 싸움이 터진다. 그러나 이런 것이 모두 소박한
그들의 가슴에 잊을 수 없는 뿌리를 내리었다.

나이 먹을수록 창선이와 순남이는 서로 내외를 하게
되었다. 어떤 때는 외면을 하는 일도 있었다. 그러나 내
외를 하고 외면을 하니만치 이면의 그 무엇은 커질 뿐
이었다.

김을 매다가도 순남이가 메(먹는 풀뿌리)¹³⁾나 나시¹⁴⁾나

time together and, naturally, they became acquainted.

It was during this time when Chang-seon got to
know his wife. To borrow a street term, they fell in
love.

"Hey, would you like this? Who wants this...?"
Chang-seon would say this while his future wife,
Sun-nam, was near, raising his hand and holding
some large pieces of candy aloft. He'd bought them
for this very purpose. A short distance away, their
cows and oxen grazed.

"Me!"

"No, me!" Children cried over each other.

"Here, Sun-nam. You asked first." No matter
whoever had really asked first, Chang-seon always
gave a couple to Sun-nam and shoved the rest into
his own mouth.

"Hey, Sun-nam, don't chew it. Just let it melt.
Shall we bet who can keep it longer?" Chang-seon
would say.

Then, other children envied them, their mouths
watery.

"That little fart is cheating. I asked first."

"He's right. He said first. And I was the next...

달뇌(모두 먹는 풀)[15] 캐러 나온 것을 있기만 하면 사람 보지 않는 틈을 타서 그리로 간다.

"뭘 캐니? 메냐?"

"메를 캐는 기 별로 없거든…… 깊이 파야 모래 속에 있는데."

순남이는 흘깃 보고는 고개를 반쯤 돌린다. 말씨도 전보다 한결 점잖아지고 하는 태도도 매우 숫처녀다워졌다.

"내 캐주지…… 오늘 기녁에 먹으러 간다, 응."

"누가 오지 말라는기…… 오늘 기녁 메떡을 하겠는데."

"야 정말…… 나 꼭 간다. 그러다가 너어 집에서 욕하면 어쩌겠니."

"언제 욕먹어 쌌는기…… 와보지도 않고……."

이리하여 순박한 맘과 맘은 풀 수 없게 맺어졌다.

겨울이 되면 해사(海事) 소식이 짜— 퍼진다. 은어(도루메기)가 잡히고 명태 배가 들어오면 고기 풍년이 났다고 살판을 만났다고 남녀노소 없이 야단들이다. 아낙들은 함지를 이고 남자들은 수레를 끌고 고기받이를 다닌

What are you doing...? Is Sun-nam your wife?"

"Just wait and see. I'll tell Sun-nam's mom!"

The children jabbered and complained.

Then, Sun-nam would get upset and yell, "Hey, you bastard—whose wife? What wife...? You bastard, are you gonna tell my mom, now? Didn't you receive a ground cherry from Ssangdol yesterday?"

"You, asshole, when did I do that?"

Then, there erupted a broil. But, these sorts of episodes took root unforgettably in their simple hearts.

As they grew older, Chang-seon and Sun-nam distanced themselves from each other. Sometimes, they even turned away when the other approached. But, the more they distanced themselves and turned away from each other, the bigger that little something grew in their hearts.

Whenever Chang-seon saw Sun-nam dig edible roots like *mes,* or pick edible plants like *nasi* and *dalnui,* while he was weeding, he went to her while other people weren't looking.

"What are you digging? Is that *mes?*"

"I'm digging *mes,* but there isn't a lot... You have to dig deep into the sand." After glancing at Chang-seon, Sun-nam immediately turned away, though.

다. 해변에 몰린다. 순남이도 해마다 그리로 다녔다. 늘 창선이네 배에 가서 사오곤 하였다. 창선이는 자기 집 고깃배만 포구에 들어오면 부리나케 나가서 고기팔이를 한다. 가장 기쁜 생각으로—그것은 날마다 순남이가 오는 까닭이다. 그 일 하는 것이 그에게는 가장 기쁨이 되었다. 은근한 희망이 따르는 까닭이다. 그는 새벽부터 신이 나서 고기를 세어 넘긴다.

"한 드럼에 얼마요?"

고기받이꾼이 이렇게 물으면,

"석 냥(육십 전)어치면 목대가 부러지오."

"알[卵]이 잘 들었소?"

"알이라니…… 고지[16], 애[17]만 떼먹어도 큰 장사죠."

"석 드럼만 세어 놓소."

"세어 주오."

이렇게 아낙네와 수레꾼이 나도 나도 때도투며 사들간다.

"하나이요, 둘이에…… 열이요…… 이렇나니 한 드럼…… 자아, 세 마리 넘어가오."

창선은 아직 나이 젊고 고기 다루는 데 익숙지 못해

Her manner of speech became gentler and her attitude towards him became more like that of a virgin.

"I'll help you... I'll come to your house to eat some this evening. Okay?"

"Who told you not to...? We're making pancakes with *mes* this evening."

"Hey, honestly... I really will come! But, what if your parents scold me?"

"When have they ever scolded you...? You've never even visited us..."

This was how the two innocent hearts became inseparably entangled.

In winter, fishing news spread quickly to the village. When the boats came back with sweetfish and walleye pollack harvest, all of the villagers, regardless of age or sex, were busy and excited at the prospect of a bumper harvest year. Women with large scooped wooden bowls on their heads and men pulling wagons rushed to the pier to buy the fish. Sun-nam went to the pier every year. She would always buy fish from Chang-seon's family boat. Whenever Chang-seon's father arrived at the pier, Chang-seon rushed to the boat to sell fish. He ran to the pier, elated, barely able to contain his

서 흔히 아낙네 것만 세곤 하였다. 한 차례 세고 이마에 땀이 추투루해서 느른한 허리를 펴며 고개를 들면 그을거리는 아낙네 틈에는 순남이가 끼여 있다. 고기 세는 사람이 한둘이 아니니까 순남이는 똑바로 그의 앞에 함지를 내려놓지 못하고 그저 그의 앞 비슷하게 비스듬히 내려놓고는 발끝도 내려다보다가는 가없는 너른 바다에 말없이 시선을 주기도 한다. 그의 얼굴은 어쩐지 좀 붉어지는 듯했다. 창선이는 비쭉 웃고 명태 중에도 알잘 든 놈을 골라가며 찍개로 척척 찍어 그의 함지에 세어 놓는다. 어물어물 한 드럼에 예닐곱 마리씩은 더 넘겨준다.

이렇게 애든 이 고장이요, 이렇게 친한 이 바다이다.

그러나 지금은 모든 것이 달라졌다. 산도 그렇고 물도 그렇다. 철도길이 고개를 갈라 먹고 창리 포구에 어선이 끊어졌다. 구수한 흙냄새 나는 마을이 없어지고 맵짠 쇠냄새 나는 공장과 벽돌집이 거만스러이 배를 붙이고 있다. 소수레가 끊어지고 부수레(기차)가 왱왱거린다. 농군은 산비탈 으슥한 곳으로 밀려가고 노가다(노동자) 패가 제노라고 쏘다닌다. 땅은 석탄 먼지에 꺼멓게

excitement at seeing Sun-nam, who went every time. Selling fish became his most favorite activity because of this secret hope. When Chang-seon counted fish for his customers at dawn, he was excited.

"How much is a score of this?" a customer would ask.

"You'll break your wrists if you buy three-*nyang* (sixty *jeon*)'s worth," Chang-seon would say.

"Do they have roe?" the customer would ask again.

"Roe? You're profiting greatly even if you just eat the testicles and entrails."

"I'll take three scores."

"I'll take a few too!" small crowds of other customers—women with their bowls and men with their wagons—all rushed to buy.

"One, two... ten... a score... here, take three more!" Chang-seon counted and handed the fish over to customers.

Because Chang-seon was still young and unskilled in dealing with fish, he handled only female customers. Sweat shining on his forehead, Chang-seon stood straight again after counting fish for customers; he could see Sun-nam glimmering

절고 배따라기 요란하던 포구는 파도 소리 홀로 쓸쓸하다. 그의 눈에는 땅도 바다도 한결같이 죽은 듯했다. 기계간 벽돌집 쇠사슬 떼굴뚝이 아무리 야단스러워도 그저 하잘것없는 까닭 모를 것이었다.

내외는 철도 둑을 넘어 고개턱에 올라섰다. 새로 이사 간 고향이 보인다. 저— 바닷가에— 그러나 옛날 구룡리 마을은 아주 말 아니다. 철도길 바람에 마을 한복판이 툭 끊어져버렸다. 마을 어귀를 파수 보던 소나무들이 늙은이 앞니같이 뭉청 빠져버렸다. 기차 굴뚝에서 나온 조그만 석탄불이 집어삼킨 불탄 두세 집이 보인다. 나직나직한 곤돌초막은 무서운 듯이 쪼그리고 있다. 자꾸 더 쪼그릴 것 같다. 그리 되면 그 속의 식구들이 모조리 깔리고 말 것이다. 창선의 머리에는 낮꿈 같은 야릇한 상상이 그려졌다—기운찬 사나이만 쪼그라진 그 지붕을 뚫고 머리를 반쯤 내민 것이 보인다. 늙은이 아낙네 어린것이 그 밑에 깔려서 숨이 팔딱거리는 것이 보인다—

창리에서 이사 간 집들은 생소한 그 서슬에 정떨어진 듯이 저— 바다 한가에 물러가 있다. 그러나 사정없는

amongst the many women. As there were many fish-counters in front of her, Sun-nam didn't dare to bring her bowl directly before Chang-seon. She pushed her bowl in Chang-seon's direction and then would stare down at her own feet or towards the vast sea. She always seemed to be blushing a little. Chang-seon grinned and hooked only roe-laden fish for her, counting each one and placing them carefully down into her bowl. He would usually give six or seven fishes more per score without a word.

It was in this very place that they had had all those anxious moments and it was in front of this very sea that they had grown in affection for each other.

But, everything had changed now—both the mountains and the sea. Railway tracks cut across the mountain pass and fishing boats had disappeared from the Chang-ri port. The village with its sweet earthy smell had disappeared and in its place, factories with a harsh metal smell stood proudly face to face with rows of brick buildings. The oxcarts had disappeared and steel carts (trains) were whirring noisily. The farmers had been driven to secluded mountain slopes and now it was the

바닷물이 삼킬 것 같다. 그래도 바닷가 사람에게는 낯선 기차에 비해서 바다가 정다웠던 모양이다.

"저기 가서 원밀석[海嘯]이 무섭지도 않나!"

"바다가 가까워서 고기받이는 제일이겠소. 그래도—"

아낙은 고기받이할 것만 생각하였다.

"되놈의 땅에서 생선을 못 먹어 창자에 탈이 났는데."

"돈만 있어 보지. 되땅이 아니라 생국[西洋] 가도 태평이지."

내외는 이런 얘기를 하며 형의 집을 찾으려고 물어볼 사람을 찾으나 좀처럼 만날 수가 없었다. 겨울이 되면 더 사람이 많이 나다닐 터인데 이상한 일이었다. 고기만 잘 잡힌다면 벌써 오는 길에서 고기받이 아낙네와 수레꾼들을 많이 만났을 것이다. 그러나 하나도 못 보았다.

3

창선이가 길가 어떤 아이에게 물어가지고 형의 집에 찾아온 때는 좀 어두컴컴했다. 어머니는 누더기를 쓰고

38

laborers strutting through the streets. The soil had been blackened with coal dust, and only the waves splashed desolately against the piers where the loud Baettaragi tunes had once been heard. To Chang-seon's eyes, both the land and the sea seemed to have died. No matter how great the machine workshops, brick buildings, and flocks of iron-chained chimneys were, they were trifling, purposeless objects to him.

The husband and wife crossed the railway banks and arrived at the head of a slope. They could see their newly moved home village far away near the sea. But good old Guryong-ri also looked terrible. The center of village had been cut in half to make way for railway tracks. The pine tree grove guarding the village at its entrance had lost trees in its center and looked like the mouth of an elderly man missing his front teeth. There were also several burned-down houses nearby. They had caught fire from the coal flame that had flown out of train chimneys. Low hamlets squatted near the ground as if frightened. They looked like they would continue shrinking more and more within themselves. Eventually, every family member of the hamlet would find themselves flattened. Chang-seon had a

가마목[18]에 드러누웠고 조카 남매는 희미한 등경불[19]
아래에서 감자떡을 치고 있었다.

"어머니, 창선입니다."

"어머니……."

내외는 바당문[20]을 열고 들어서자 성큼 정주에 올라
서며 어머니 앞에 절을 넙석 하였다.

"아니, 창선이라니……."

어머니는 너무도 놀라고 반가웠던 것이다.

"어머니, 그새 소환[21]이나 안 계셨습니까…… 댁내가
다 무고한가요."

"응…… 원…… 이 추운데 그래 살아 왔구나."

어머니는 곱[22]이 낀 눈을 슴벅거리며[23] 자세히 쳐다
본다. 어머니 아니고는 날 수 없는 눈물이 고였다.

"죽잖으면 그래도 만나는구나…… 아들을 낳다지. 어
디 보자…… 이름은 무엇이라고 지었니?"

"간도에서 났다고 간남이라고 했습니다…… 추위에
감기를 만나서…… 영 죽게 되었어요."

아낙은 젖에서 어린것을 떼어 어머니에게 안겨 드렸
다.

strange daydream-like vision: A sturdy-looking man's head was peeking through a hole in a collapsed roof while elderly folk, women, and children all panting beneath it.

Houses that had moved from Chang-ri had gathered some distance away, near the sea, as if they had become disgusted by this strange, fierce new environment. As such, they looked as if they would soon be swallowed by the ruthless waves of the sea. All the same, they must have found the sea friendlier than the stream of unfamiliar trains; they'd once lived near the sea, after all.

"So close to the sea... My, aren't they afraid of tsunamis?" Chang-seon wondered aloud.

"They're so close to the sea, they could unload the fish easily." His wife thought only of getting fish.

"We had stomach trouble in the Chinks' land because we couldn't eat fish."

"If only we had money! Then, we'd be fine not only in China but also in the Western countries."

The husband and wife continued to chat while looking for someone to ask about Chang-seon's brother's house—but all to no avail. This was very strange, because, usually in winter, there would be

"아이구, 컸구나…… 이런 무겁기라구…… 작년 구
월에 났다지…… 원 늙은것은 얼른 가고 너희나 잘 살
아야겠는데……."

어머니 눈에서는 눈물이 굴러 떨어졌다.

"그래 그곳 사는 일이 어떻더냐. 예보다는 좋다더구
나."

"말 마십시오. 죽지 않은 게 천만다행입니다. 되놈들
등쌀에 몰려다니기에 볼일을 못 봅니다. 우리 살던 고
장에서도 쉰 아무 집 되는 데서 벌써 열 집이나 어디로
떠났습니다. 무지막지하게 땅을 떼고 몰아내는 데야 어
찌합니까…… 우리 동리 아래 동리 영남 사람은 한 집
이 몰살을 했답니다."

"저런…… 몰살은…… 끔찍도 해라."

"늙은 어머니와 아낙과 어린 자식들을 두고 가장이
벌이를 갔더라나요. 한 게 뜻대로 되지 못해서 한 스무
날 만에야 돌아와 보니 늙은이가 방에서 얼어 죽고 아
낙은 어디로 갔는지 보이지 않더래요."

"저런…… 청인이 채갔나? 원…… 사람은 못 살 데로
구나."

more pedestrians around than other seasons. If there had been a good catch, they would have already met women and wagoners buying fish. But they hadn't run into even a single soul.

3

When Chang-seon finally ran into a child on the street and arrived at his brother's house, it was growing dark outside. Mother lay near the hearth under a tattered blanket and Chang-seon's nephew and niece were pounding potatoes into cakes under a dimly lit lamp.

"Mother, it's me, Chang-seon."

"Mother..."

Chang-seon and Sun-nam opened the kitchen door, rushed to the floor, and kowtowed to Chang-seon's mother.

"Why—Chang-seon!" Mother said. She was very surprised and glad.

"Mother, how have you been? How is everyone in the family?"

"Oh... hm... You survived such cold weather and

"그런 게 아닌데, 가장도 처음은 그렇게 생각했답니다…… 그래서 칼을 들고 찾아 나섰대요."

"죽일라고, 원 저런…… 치가 떨리는 일이라구는."

"남편이 미친 사람같이 두루 찾아다니는데 눈얼음 속에 사람 같은 것이 보이더래요…… 그래 막상 가보니 아낙이 옳더라지요."

"아, 그래 살았어?"

"아니…… 눈 속에서 얼어 죽었는데 머리에는 강냉이(옥수수) 한 되를 이고 어린애는 하나는 업고 하나는 앞에 안은 채 얼어붙었더래요."

"원, 하늘도 무심하지. 그것들이 무슨 죄가 있다구."

"그뿐인가요. 남편까지 죽었답니다. 발광이 나서……."

"사람은 못 살 데다. 말도 마라. 원, 끔찍끔찍해서 그걸 누가 듣는단 말이냐…… 그래도 쟤 애비(창선의 형)는 정 안 되면 그리로 간다구…… 원, 하느님 맙소사."

"소문만 듣고 갔다가는 큰일납니다. 그렇게 죽고 몰려다니는 사람이 부지기수랍니다. 여북해서 이 겨울에 나왔겠습니까."

returned safely."

Mother looked at them carefully, blinking her grit-encrusted eyes. Her eyes were filled with tears, the kind only a mother would shed.

"We've lived on and now we're able to meet again... I heard that you had a son. Let me see him... What's his name?"

"We call him Gan-nam because he was born in Gando [Jiandao]... He caught a cold because of the cold weather... he almost died."

Sun-nam took the baby from her breast and handed it to her mother-in-law.

"Wow! He's grown quite a bit. So heavy. I heard he was born in September last year. Huh, the old need be go quickly so that you can live well."

Teardrops rolled down from Mother's eyes.

"So, how was it to live up there? I hear it's better than here."

"Oh my, no no. We're extremely lucky not to have died there. The Chinks harassed us so much that it was impossible for us to try anything. Ten out of more than fifty families already left the area where we lived. What could you do when they'd ruthlessly snatch your land from right under you and drive you out? An entire family from Yeongnam died in a

"엔들[24] 여북하겠니. 생불여사다…… 오늘도 어쩌면 살아볼까 몰려들 가더라만—"

"참, 형님 읍으로 갔대지요. 아주머니까지……."

"설상가상이다. 살다 살다 안 되니 오늘 감사라든지 난 모른다만 그리로 온 동리가 몰려갔다더라."

"감사? 무슨 때문에요?"

"원, 세월이 없구나. 보지 못하니 태평이지. 모두 굶어 죽는다고 야단들이다."

"글쎄, 그렇다기로 도장관이 살려 주겠습니까."

"사흘 굶은 범이 원을 가리겠니. 죽을 판인데…… 고기가 잡혀야 살지. 무얼 먹고 산단 말이냐."

"고기가 안 잡히는데 누구를 치탈하겠습니까. 세월 탓이지요."

"세월 탓이 아니라는구나. 포구가 나빠서 그렇단다. 배도 못 뭇고[25] 뭇으면 마사진다는구나……[26] 시월에 모래언덕 집 유새네 은어(도루메기) 배가 마사졌다. 사람이 셋이 고기밥이 되었단다. 그 집 맏사람이 분김에 회사에 가서 행렬을 하다가 ×××한테 몰려나고 술이 잔뜩 취해서 마사진 배 조각을 두드리고 통곡하다가 얼어

village south of ours."

"Oh... an entire family... how horrifying!"

"The man went away to make money, leaving his elderly mother, wife, and young children behind. As things didn't go as he had hoped, he returned about twenty days later and found his mother frozen to death in his house and his wife missing."

"Oh, no... did a Chinese man kidnap her? Huh... that's not a place for human beings."

"That wasn't exactly what happened, though the husband also thought so at first... So, he went out to look for his wife—he had a knife."

"To kill her, I guess. My, goodness... how horrendous."

"While the husband was wandering around looking for his wife like a madman, he saw a figure like a human being in the middle of frozen snow mound... When he approached it, he discovered it was his wife."

"Oh, so, he rescued her?"

"No... she died frozen in the snow, holding half a gallon of corn on her head, piggybacking a child, and holding another child in front."

"Oh, how merciless! How pitiful!"

"Not only that. In the end, even the husband died

죽었단다. 원—"

"그런데 회사는 무슨 회삽니까."

"저게 그 창리바닥을 못 봤니…… 그 ×××란다. ×
야, 원—"

"어째서요?"

"이리로 온 게 누구 때문이냐. 글쎄 창리야 좀 좋았니.
운수가 고단하면 자빠져도 코가 깨진다고…… 글쎄 그
터를 내준 게 잘못이지."

어머니 말만 들어가지고는 자세한 내용을 알기 어려
웠다. 그러나 대체 어지간한 일이 아닌 것은 짐작할 수
가 있었다. 그러나 온 동리가 쓰러져간다는 것은 암만
해도 의심쩍은 일이다.

의혹도 의혹이려니와 그러나 배가 더 고팠다. 그래서
어머니가 권하는 대로 형의 내외를 기다리는 감자밥으
로 우선 요기나 했다.

"이게 무슨 재단이 났구나. 갈 때에도 말이 많더니 왜
여태 못 오는지……."

어머니는 오래간만에 만난 기쁨이 점점 엷어지고 잠
시 잊었던 근심이 다시 시작되었다.

—of madness."

"That's not a place for human beings. Heaven forbid! Huh, how could anyone have a heart to even listen to such a terrible story? But, your brother said that he would go there if he had no alternative... Goodness, Heaven Forbid!"

"What a mistake it is to go there, just naively believing in rumors! So many people either die or are driven out like that. How miserable do you think it is over there if we decided to get out in the middle of winter?"

"It's miserable here, too! Living is worse than dying here, too... Villagers went downtown today to survive..."

"Oh, I heard that Brother went downtown. And even sister-in-law..."

"It's misfortune on top of misfortune. Things have gotten so bad that it's hard just to hang on. And so all villagers went to see the governor or someone."

"The governor? Why?"

"Well, times are so bad. Only those who don't see us can feel at peace. Everyone is crying out that they're starving to death."

"Well, even so, would the governor actually do anything to save us?"

"글쎄요, 날씨가 별안간 추워져서……."

창선이 내외도 저으기[27] 근심되었다.

"날씨도 날씨지만…… 온 별일이더라. 동리에서 몰려
나서기만 하면 어쩐지 ××이 부득부득 못 가게 한다더
구나…… 그래 오늘 아침은 장날 핑계를 대고 새벽부
터 장으로 갑네 하고 패패 떠났다…… 이제 무슨 일이
났다, 났어…… 원."

"오겠습지요. 누우십시오."

창선이는 어머니를 안심시키려도 사정을 몰라서 할
말이 나서지 않았다. 어머니는 이쪽저쪽으로 돌아누우
며 끝끝내 맘을 놓지 못하는 모양이다. 조카 남매는 새
동생을 가운데 놓고 노전[28]가지에 불을 붙여 팽팽 돌린
다, 감자떡을 떼어준다, 손장난을 맞춘다 하더니 그만
자는 체 없이 곤드라지고 말았다. 아낙도 어린것을 끼
고 노그라져버렸다.[29]

4

창선의 형 창룡이 내외가 집에 돌아온 것은 밤이 매

"Would a tiger starving for three days fear a magistrate? Especially when it's right about to die?" Mother said, "The only way we can live is if we can catch fish, y'know. How are we supposed to survive without fish?"

"If fish don't come, who's to blame? These are just hard times, aren't they?"

"I heard that it's actually not just the times. It's because of the poor condition of the port. It's impossible for boats to enter the port and even when they do, they'd just break... The Yusae's family's sweetfish boat that used to stay on top of the sand hill broke last October. Three of the people on board became fish food. The eldest of the brothers was so enraged that he went to the company and made a row only to be dragged out by xxx. Then, completely drunken, he wailed and pounded the broken boat, and ended up freezing to death. My..."

"You mentioned some company—but what is this company?"

"Well, there, haven't you seen Chang-ri?" Mother continued, "That's the xxx company. It's x. Damn..."

"What happened?"

"Who drove us here? You remember how great Chang-ri was, don't you? They say the bread al-

우 이슥한 때였다.

"온 어쩌면 이렇게 변하였습니까. 영 딴 세상 같습니다."

피차 오래간만에 만난 회포 인사가 끝나자 창선은 간도 형편을 대강 말하고는 이렇게 말하였다.

"말 말게. 냉수에 이 부러질 노릇이지…… 한둘도 아니요 온 동리가 기지사경(幾至死境)이네…… 그래 이 소식도 못 들었나? 신문사라고 신문사는 다 왔다 갔네."

"글쎄 어머니에게서 대강 들었습니다만…… 아주 금시초문이지 들을 길이 있습니까."

창룡이는 처음 ××××××가 될 때 형편을 얘기하였다. 이 근방 토지를 매수하며 ……던 말과 그 사이에 소위 ××유력자들이 나서서 춤을 추던 야바위를 말하였다.

"이리로 옮기기만 하면 여기다 인천만 한 항구를 만들어줄 테요. 시장 학교 무슨 우편소니 큰길이니 다 내준다고…… 야단스러운 지도(地圖)를 가지고 와서 구룡리를 가리키며 제2의 인천을 보라고…… 원, 산 눈 뺄 세상이지."

ways falls on the buttered side... Well, it was our mistake to give up that village."

Chang-seon couldn't quite understand what exactly had happened from his mother's words. Still, he could guess that something extraordinary had happened. At any rate, it was quite incredible that the entire village had moved.

Although Chang-seon wanted to know what had happened, he was more hungry than curious at that moment. So, he and his wife ate some of the potato cake that had been waiting for his brother and sister-in-law, obeying his mother's urges.

"Something must have gone wrong. They left full of troubles, and I wonder why they haven't returned yet..."

Mother's happiness from seeing her son's family was gradually replaced by her resumed worries.

"Well, the weather suddenly turned cold..."

Chang-seon and Sun-nam also looked very worried.

"The weather's one thing, but... Things are so strange. I heard that whenever villagers gathered to go downtown, for some reason xx tries to prevent them from going ... So, the villagers left in twos and threes early this morning, pretending to go to the

"그래서요?"

"그래도 이천 명이나 되니 그리 얼른 ×겠나. 해서 구
룡리에다 창리만 한 설비를 해주면 간다고 했지……
그리고 우리도 한 집이라도 먼저 가면 ……인다고 온
동리에서 말이 됐지. …… 했더니 ……에서도 아주 능
청스럽게 그렇게 하라구 호언장담을 하더니…… 온 이
런 놈의 야바위가 있나. 그렇게 말해 놓고는 뒤로 한 사
람씩 파는구만."

"파다니요?"

"파는 놈이 병신이지. 저 우물 녘 집 개 수경이 있지
않나. 사람이 붙어야 하지. ××에서 꾀군을 그리로 보
냈더래. 커다란 봉투에 무엇을 수북이 넣어서 맡기어
장차 장자가 되는 봉투라고…… 우선 구룡리로 옮기기
만 하면 그 봉투를 줄 텐데 잘 간수했다가 떼어보면 알
조가 있다구."

"무슨 봉투래요. 사실이던가요?"

"무얼 사실이야. 엊그제야 떼어보니 십 원짜리 한 장
인가 들었더래…… 그래도 그 바람에 신이 나서 동리
약속을 깨트리고 먼저 옮았네그려. 죽을 힘 쳤겠지. 그

fair... Something must have gone wrong. It must have—Hm!"

"I'm sure they'll be back sooner or later. Please lie down, Mother."

Although Chang-seon wanted to reassure his mother, he didn't know what to say; he still wasn't sure he understood what was going on. Mother tossed and turned, clearly anxious. Chang-seon's nephew and niece were trying to play with their newly acquainted baby cousin lying in between them. They lit and spun straw from a straw mat with him, fed him a piece of potato cake, and made hand gestures to entertain him. Shortly, he fell asleep on the spot. Sun-nam also collapsed, holding their baby in her arms.

4

It was very late at night when Chang-seon's brother Chang-ryong and his wife returned.

"My, how could things have changed so much? This seems like a whole different world," said Chang-seon after exchanging greetings and telling

러나 동리 터에 그걸 죽이나 어쩌나…… 하더니 구수

한 풍설에 한 집 두 집 설비도 해주기 전에 그만 다 옮

아버렸네그려."

"집값은 다 받았겠지요?"

"그야 받았지만 그걸 가지고 뭘 하나. 고기가 잡혀야

말이지…… 워낙 금년은 어산이 말 아니네."

"아주 그렇게 안 잡힙니까."

"아따, 이 포구를 못 봤나…… 축항인지 무언지 해준

다던 게 그래논 꼴만 보게. 큰 집 마당만 하게 좌우 쪽에

쉰 아무 발씩 방축을 처쌓았다네. 거기에 무슨 배를 매

며…… 벌써 일 년도 못 돼서 마흔다섯 척 중에서 아홉

채가 바사졌네.[30] 저 류 관청네와 모래언덕 집과……."

"그건 들었습니다만 사람까지 상패가 났다니……."

"글쎄 여보게, 서호에 가서 받아오면 명태 한 바리에

스무 냥(사 원)은 더 주어야 하네. 한데도 서호 다니는

길은 돌강스랭이[31]가 되어서 많이 이고 다닐 수도 없고

수렛길이 없어서 수레도 못 다니고…… 게다가 해풍이

심해서 고기받이꾼이 얼마를 얼어 죽을지 모르네. 그래

누누이 회사에 말을 했건만 영 막무가내하구만."

him how his life had been in Jiandao.

"Goodness gracious, it's been absolutely mad... Not just one or two families, but the entire village is about to starve to death... So, you hadn't heard about it? Reporters from all the newspaper companies in the country have been here."

"Well, I've just heard a little from Mother... but this is my first time hearing about it. How could I have known?"

Chang-ryong explained how xxxxxx had first come to the village and began to buy lands and xxx villagers out, how so-called xx potentates played off a fraud upon them.

"If we moved here, they promised to build a large port city like Incheon. With markets, schools, post offices and large roads, you know. They showed us a flashy map and pointed to Guryong-ri, called it the second Incheon. Goodness, this is the kind of world where they'd pull your eyeballs out even while you were looking at them."

"So what happened?"

"There's about two thousand people here, so how could we all move to x so quickly? So, we said that we'd all move if they first built what we had in Chang-ri in Guryong-ri, at least... And then

"저런 ……는 ……그걸 ……두어요."

"애초에 도청에서 설계를 했느니 저이는 그대로만 했
으니 모른다는 게지…… 그래 오늘은 ××× 있는 데
로 가보았네…… ××× 나와서 가라구만 하지 어디
꼴이나 볼 수 있나."

"그래, 못 만났어요?"

"석양에야 겨우 만나긴 했네. 잘 해준다고 하게 다지
고 왔지만……."

"그런데 아낙들까지…… 난립니다. 바로─"

"제 발등이 따구니까[32] 가지 말래도 가는 게지. 또 그
래야 관청에서도 알아주네. 여기 번영회라는 게 있어
가지고 대표가 4, 5차 나가도 돌아가서 기다리라고만
하지 어디 하나나 해주나. 해서 이번은 대표도 소용없
다 모두 가자 하고 간 걸세."

"그럼 인제는 잘될 모양입니까?"

"말만은 고맙데…… 한데 워낙 이제부터는 바다가 깊
어서 한 간에 몇 만 원씩 든다네그려."

"그래도 회사에서 으레 해놓아야지 별수 있습니까. 안
해주면 우리 동리를 도로 달라지요."

we all agreed that, if one family moved first, we wouldn't follow. We'd only go together. And so xx, unfazed, cunningly declaring that we should do as we pleased. But—what swindlers! After that, they began to scam the villagers one by one behind all of our backs."

"Scam?"

"Everyone who was scammed was stupid. You know Su-gyeong? He lives in the house near the well, right? You had to be smart. It turns out that xx sent one of their men to his house. That man brought him a large envelope full of something, saying that it was going to make him wealthy... They told him that if he first moved to Guryong-ri, they'd give him that envelope, that he should keep it safe and that once he opened it, he would know what they meant."

"So what was in that envelope? Were they telling the truth?"

"Truth my ass! He said that he had opened it only a few days ago to find only a ten-*won* note... Still, believing their promise, he broke our villagers' promise and moved first. He might have thought that it was do or die. But, what could we do to him? Kill him? Then, one by the one, all villagers

"원, 가당치도 않은 ……가 우리말은 고사하고 ××도 네뚜리[33]만치 안다네. 원, 영의정을 업고 다니는지 그 ×× 등쌀은 같은 장수가 없데그려. 돈이면 그만이야. 정승이 부럽겠나 ××× 무섭겠나. 무에 무서울 게 있어야 말이지…… 저 관사만 보게…… 명함도 못 들이겠데. 뽕― 하면 자동차라고."

자리에 누워서까지 이런 얘기를 하는 사이에 창선은 그만 곤해서 어느새 코를 골았다. 그러나 창룡이는 이 궁리 저 궁리에 새날이 오도록 잠이 들지 않았다. 그에게는 무거운 짐 한 짝이 더 얹히었다.

5

창선이는 한심스러운 생각이 더쳐왔다. 제 고장이라고 그리워하였고 제 친족이라고 찾아는 왔으나 생각던 바와는 아주 천양지판이다. 조선 가면 아무 일이라도 해먹으려니 했으나 막상 와보니 그 '아무 일'이란 아무데서도 찾을 수 없었다. 일하고 싶어도 할 일이 없고 힘을 쓸래도 쓸 곳이 없고 고기도 잡아먹을 수 없고 농사

began to move, deceived by the sweet rumors, until we all ended up here before any of the promised facilities were built."

"I suppose you all received the compensation payments for your houses?"

"Of course, we received them, but what could we do with them? We have to catch fish to live... This year was a bad year."

"So, no catches at all?"

"My—didn't you see the port?" Chang-ryong continued, "Look what they did after promising to harbor construction. It's only the size of a backyard of a large house. They built only fifty or so feet banks to the left and right. Where are we supposed to moor our boats? Within less than a year, already nine out of forty-five boats broke. That officer Ryu and the family on the sand hill..."

"I heard about that, but it's terrible that people have been hurt and have even died..."

"Well, if you go to Seoho to buy walleye pollacks, you have to pay twenty *nyang* (four *won*) more per score. Even then, the road to Seoho is so rough that you can't carry many on your head. And a wagon can't pass there, either, so you can't carry them in wagons. Besides, the sea breeze is so

도 지을 수 없다. 대대로 전하여오던 손익은 일 맛들인 일은 이리하여 얻어 만날 수 없고 눈이 멀게서 산송장이 될 것만 같았다.

그러나 정든 옛일이나 그네가 같이 밀려간 자리에는 낯선 새 놀음(공장 기계)이 주인같이 타리개를 틀었다. 검은 굴뚝이 새 소리를 외치고 눈 서투른 무서운 공장이 새 일꾼을 찾으나 그것은 너무도 자기 몸과 거리가 먼 것 같았다. 그만치 할 일이 있고 할 뜻이 있는 옛일에 대한 애착이 아직까지 뿌리 깊이 가슴을 부여잡고 있다. 그런데 그 일은 어디 가고 꿈도 안 꾸던 뚱딴지같은 일터가 제 맘대로 벌어져 있다. 게트림을 하면서 턱으로 사람을 부린다. 없는 사람을—그러나 차마 발이 떨어지지 않는다. 천하없어도 후려 넣는 절대명령이요 울며불며라도 가찮을 수 없는 그곳이언만— 이리하여 망설이는 과도기의 공포와 설움이 그의 가슴을 쑤시었다.

구룡리 백성의 살림은 더욱 말 아니었다. 겨울이 가고 봄이 오는 사이에 쌀독의 낟알은 죄다 없어졌다. 겟덕(물고기 말리는 말뚝)은 부엌이 다 집어먹었다. 그래도 잘해 준다던 소식은 찾아오지 않았다. 포구에는 배따라기

harsh I wonder how many fish buyers would end up freezing to death on their way to Seoho and back. So, we've complained to the company again and again, but to no avail."

"My goodness, and xx just left them alone?"

"They claim that they don't know what more they have to do because they followed the blueprint offered by the provincial office faithfully... So we all went to see xxx today... But xxx just told us to leave. We weren't even able to see anyone's face."

"So, you couldn't meet him?"

"It was only as the sun was setting that we were able to meet him. We'd insisted firmly and had him made promise to take care of matters before we came back, but..."

"So, even the women... what trouble! Just..."

"The women feel our pain, too. Even though we told them not to, they insisted. Besides, it's only when the women show up does the office pay any attention. We have our Prosperity Association and the president has been to the office four or five times. But they only told him to go back and wait, and then did nothing. So this time we decided that the president alone wouldn't have any impact and that we all should go together."

가 떠보지 못하고 산야에는 격양의 노래가 끊어졌다. 다만 들리느니 저녁놀이 사라지는 황혼의 노동자 노래 뿐이다.

장진물이 넘어서 수력 전기 되고
내호 바닥 기계 속은 질소 비료가 되네

아—령 아—령 아라리가 났네
아리랑 고개로 넘겨넘겨주—소

논밭간 좋은 건 기계간이 되고
계집애 잘난 건 요리간만 가네

텁스럽고 까라진[34] 아리랑이보다—사자밥을 목에 단 배꾼의 노래보다 씩씩한 노래다. 옛 살림을 빈정대고 새 살림을 자랑하는 노래다. 그 후 얼마 못 되어서 이 고장 백성들은 상투를 자르고 공장으로 몰려갔다. 그러나 그렇게 함부로 써주는 것이 아니다. 맨 힘차고 뼈 굵고 거슬거슬하고 나이 젊은 우둥퉁하고 미욱스럽게 생긴

"So, will everything be better now?"

"They talked sweetly... But they said that the sea was so deep it would cost several tens of thousands of *won* per *gan*.[1]"

"Nevertheless, the company should take care of all of this, yes? If they don't, then we need to demand that they return our village to us."

"Oh no... that would truly be impossible... xxx not only doesn't care about what we say, but they also don't think very much of xx. They must have the prime minister in their pocket. No general could equal their power. Money is everything. Might they envy a cabinet minister or fear xxx? It'd be fine if they feared something! Just look at their official residence... You can't even leave your name card there. They say beep means a car, you know."

Chang-seon fell asleep shortly. He began to snore even as he spoke, his brother nearby in bed. But Chang-ryong could not fall asleep until dawn, pondering the various options and possibilities left to their village. Now he had one more burden on him.

사람만 뽑히었다. 그리고 거기서 까불려난 늙고 약한 사람이 개똥밭 농사나 짓고 은어 부스러기 고기잡이나 하는 수밖에 없었다. 어떤 사람은 온 가장을 보따리에 꾸둥쳐 지고 영원 장진으로 떠나갔다.

화전(火田)이나 해 먹을까 하는 것이다.

창선이는 요행 공장 노동자로 뽑혔다. 상투 자르고 감발 치고 부삽 들고 콘크리트 반죽하는 생소한 사람이 되었다.

1) 집에 두고 쓰는 세간 등의 온갖 살림 도구.
2) 보고미. 바구니의 방언.
3) 꽉 차도록 가득.
4) 나라에서 주는 녹봉.
5) 짜그리다. 짓눌러서 여기저기 고르지 않게 오그라지게 하다.
6) 발감개.
7) 후미키리(ふみきり). 건널목.
8) 아츠럽다(북한어). 신경을 자극하여 보거나 듣기에 견디기 어려울 정도로 거북하다.
9) 가지가 빈틈없이 많이 퍼져 소복하게 된 어린 소나무.
10) 참조 점심. 참조로 지은 점심밥.
11) 여비다. '여위다'의 방언(강원, 함경).
12) 아잘 것 없이. 알려고 할 것 없이.
13) 메꽃 또는 메꽃의 뿌리.
14) '냉이'의 방언(경기, 경상, 전남, 충북, 함경).
15) '달래'의 방언(강원).
16) 명태의 이리, 알, 내장을 통틀어 이르는 말.
17) 명태 따위의 간을 이르는 말(북한어).
18) 부엌과 구들 사이를 터놓은 집에서 가마가 걸려 있는 아랫목 (북한어).

5

Chang-seon was miserable. Although he'd returned to his home village and the family he'd so missed, things were as different as day and night from what he'd expected. In Chosun, he'd thought he could make his living, working at whatever jobs, but there were no jobs there whatsoever. He was willing to work, but there was no work to be had. He wanted to use his strength, but there was no use for it. He could neither fish nor farm. Nowhere could he find the kind of work his family had been trained to complete for generations. He was afraid of ending up numbered among the living dead.

But, strange new machines took up the place like its owner, the place from which fond old memories had been driven out like wanderers. Although black chimneys coughed out new sorts of cries and the giant, alien factory looked for new workers, they seemed too far away from his body. That was how deeply his love for the old work, which he was eager to resume, had taken root in his heart. But that work had disappeared and a fantastically strange new workplace, which no one had ever even

19) 등경(燈檠). 등잔걸이.

20) 부엌으로 드나드는 문(함경).

21) 소환(所患). 앓고 있는 병(북한어).

22) 눈곱.

23) 슴벅거리다. 눈꺼풀이 움직이며 눈이 자꾸 감겼다 떠졌다 하다. 또는 그렇게 되게 하다.

24) 여긴들.

25) 뭇다. 여러 조각을 한데 붙이거나 이어서 어떠한 물건을 만들다.

26) 마사지다. 부서지거나 깨져서 못쓰게 되다.

27) '적이(꽤 어지간한 정도로)'의 북한어.

28) 갈잎이나 조짚(북한어).

29) 노그라지다. 맥이 빠지고 축 늘어지다.

30) '바서지다'의 북한어.

31) 강스랭이. 가시랭이. 풀이나 나무의 가시 부스러기.

32) '따갑다'의 방언(강원, 황해).

33) 사람이나 물건 따위를 대수롭지 않게 여기다.

34) 까라지다. 기운이 빠져 축 늘어지다.

* 작가 고유의 문체나 당시 쓰이던 용어를 그대로 살려 원문에 최대한 가깝게 표기하고자 하였다. 단, 현재 쓰이지 않는 말이나 띄어쓰기는 현행 맞춤법에 맞게 표기하였다.

《조선지광》, 1929

dreamt of, was rising. That workplace called them, leisurely belching out its fumes—those who owned nothing. And yet, Chang-seon found it hard to force himself to go there. But its call was an absolute call he couldn't help going even if he had to go kicking and screaming... Thus, fear and sorrow pricked and pained his heart.

Living in Guryong-ri worsened by the day. As winter turned to spring, they exhausted the grains from their rice jars. Every fish-drying stick was swallowed up in the kitchen fire. Still, no news of the promised improvement came. Baettaragi song couldn't float in the air of the port, and farming songs disappeared from the hills and fields. The only songs one heard now were worker songs around sunset.

Jangjin water overflows to become hydroelectricity;
Inner Lake bottom becomes nitrogenous fertilizer inside a machine.

A-ryeong A-ryeong Arariga natne.
Send me away over the Arirang Pass.

Good farms and fields become machine workshops;

Pretty girls have only restaurants to go.

This song had more life than the hardy and
mournful Arirang Song or the fishermen's song that
always had death hanging over it. This new song
made fun of the old way of life and boasted of the
new. Soon enough, the people in the area had their
topknots shorn and went to the factory. They
weren't all readily hired. Only the strong, large-
boned, rough, young, plump, and simple-minded
men were selected. The old and weak who weren't
hired, had no other choice but to farm in barren
fields and fishing for the few sweetfish they could
find. Some packed all their household goods and
left for Yeongwon and Jangjin.

They were planning to plant after burning off
their fields in the mountains.

Luckily, Chang-seon was selected as a factory
worker. He had his topknot cut, wrapped his feet
with bandages, and became that strange man who
would now take a shovel and knead the concrete.

1) A *gan* is a unit equivalent of 6 square feet.

Translated by Jeon Seung-hee

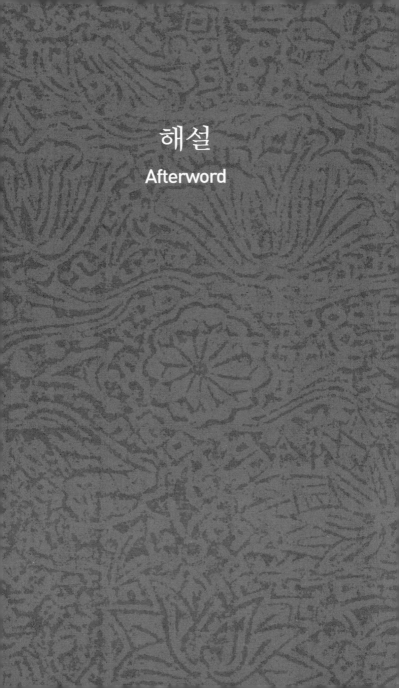

해설

Afterword

식민지 조선에서 일어난 본원적
축적 과정의 재현

이경재 (문학평론가)

「과도기」(過渡期, 《조선지광》, 1929.4.)는 "캐피탈리즘의 필연한 발전상에 따른 농촌의 몰락과 기계공업도시의 발흥, 따라서 농민의 노동자화라는 인간생활의 과도기를 그린 것이다."(「문예시감」, 《문예공론》 2호, 1929.6., 80~81쪽)라는 작가의 말(의도)이 훌륭하게 예술적으로 구현된 작품이다. 이 작품의 핵심적인 초점자는 살기 위해 간도로 떠났다가 그곳에서도 버텨내지 못하고 4년 만에 고향에 돌아온 창선이다. 한동안 고향을 떠났던 창선이의 시각을 통하여 그동안 이루어진 고향 마을의 변화는 좀 더 뚜렷하게 부각된다. 「과도기」의 서사는 4년 만에 고향에 돌아온 창선이 평화롭던 고향 마을이 황폐한 공

Representation of Primitive Accumulation Process in Colonial Chosun

Lee Kyung-jae (literary critic)

According to the author's own words, "Transition" (originally published in *Chosunjigwang* April 1929 issue) "describes the transitional phase of our lives—the collapse of agriculture and the rise of the mechanical and industrial city as well as the transformation of farmers into factory workers—all of which accompany the inevitable development of capitalism" ("Munyesigam," in *Munyegongron* 2 [June 1929] 80~81). The protagonist of this story is Chang-seon who returns to his hometown from Jiandao, driven back after miserable four-year hiatus. When he returns, the change in his hometown is especially striking in Chang-seon's eyes:

장지대로 변한 것을 확인하고, 그 시대적 흐름에 맞춰 공장노동자가 되기까지의 과정으로 정리해 볼 수 있다.

이러케 애든 이 고장이요. 이러케 친한 이 바다이다.

그러나 지금은 모든 것이 달나젓다. 산도 그러코 물도 그러타. 철도ㅅ길이 고개를 갈나 먹고 창리 포구에 어선이 슨어젓다. 구수한 흙냄새 나는 마을이 업서지고 맵짠 쇠냄새 나는 공장과 벽돌집이 거만스러히 배를 부치고 잇다. 소 수레가 슨어지고 부수레(긔차)가 왱왱그런다. 농군은 산비탈 으슥한 곳으로 밀녀가고 노가다(로동자) 패가 제노라고 쏘댄닌다. 쌍은 석탄 몬지에 썸엇케 절고 배싸라기 요란하든 포구는 파도ㅅ소리 홀노 쓸쓸하다. 그의 눈에는 쌍도 바다도 한결가티 죽은 듯햇다. 긔게ㅅ간 벽돌집 쇠사슬 쎄굴쑥이 아모리 야단스러워도 그저 하잘 것 업는 까닭 모를 것이엿다.

위의 인용문에서 과거의 창리와 현재의 창리는 수사적인 차원에서부터 차별적으로 묘사된다. 과거의 창리는 '애든' '친한' '구수한'과 같이 긍정적인 어휘로 표현되는 데 반해, 현재의 창리는 '맵짠' '거만스러히' '왱왱그런

It was in this very place that they had had all those anxious moments and it was in front of this very sea that they had grown in affection for each other.

But, everything had changed now—both the mountains and the sea. Railway tracks cut across the mountain pass and fishing boats had disappeared from the Chang-ri port. The village with its sweet earthy smell had disappeared and in its place, factories with a harsh metal smell stood proudly face to face with rows of brick buildings. The oxcarts had disappeared and steel carts (trains) were whirring noisily. The farmers had been driven to secluded mountain slopes and now it was the laborers strutting through the streets. The soil had been blackened with coal dust, and only the waves splashed desolately against the piers where the loud Baettaragi tunes had once been heard. To Chang-seon's eyes, both the land and the sea seemed to have died. No matter how great the machine workshops, brick buildings, and flocks of iron-chained chimneys were, they were trifling, purposeless objects to him.

In this passage, the Chang-ri of the past and the

다' '쏘댄닌다' '쓸쓸하다' '죽은 듯'과 같은 부정적인 어휘로 표현되고 있음을 확인할 수 있다. 이것은 자본과 권력의 결탁에 의해 자본주의화 되어 가는 현실에 대한 작가의 비판적 인식이 표현된 결과라고 할 수 있다. 또한 자본과 권력은 구룡리에 시장, 학교, 우편소 등이 갖추어진 "제이의 인천"을 만들어 주겠다며, 창리 사람들을 구룡리로 강제 이주시켰지만 그들은 어떤 약속도 지키지 않는다. 오히려 구룡리에서는 부실공사로 지어진 포구로 인해 배가 자주 부서지고 고기도 잡히지 않는다. 이제 사람들은 과거와 같은 삶의 방식을 고수해서는 생존마저 위협받는 상황에 처한 것이다. 전통적인 조선의 농어촌은 자본과 권력의 힘에 의해 와해되고, 사람들은 어쩔 수 없이 가난한 임금노동자가 되어 고단한 삶을 이어가게 된다.

「과도기」에서 창리 마을 사람들이 겪는 일들은 마르크스가 자본주의 발전의 초기 단계에 존재한다고 주장한 본원적 축적(primitive accumulation)의 과정에 해당한다. 마르크스는 자본주의를 발전시키기 위해서는 생산자(농민이나 수공업자)를 그들의 생산수단(토지)으로부터 분리하는 과정이 전제되어야 한다고 보았다. 이러한 과

Chang-ri of the present are described markedly differently. The Chang-ri of the past is an overwhelmingly positive place where love grew and where one could smell a sweet earthy smell. The Chang-ri of the present, though, is surrounded by a "harsh metal smell" and a "whirring noise," and it is a "proud" and "desolate" place. This contrast reflects the author's critical attitude towards the capitalization process underway enacted by the consolidated forces of the authorities and capitalists. Chang-seon discovers the capitalists and authorities lied when they drove villagers out of their home village with sweet promises of a "second Incheon," a new village marked by new markets, schools, and post offices. In Guryong-ri, the villagers can no longer survive in their accustomed way of fishing and farming, their boats broken and their fishing facilities pathetic and haphazardly constructed. The combined power of capitalists and authorities has destroyed the traditional farming and fishing villages and the people now have no choice but to become destitute wage laborers.

What the villagers of Chang-ri are experiencing is the "primitive accumulation" stage, what Marx argued to be the early stage of capitalist develop-

정을 통해서만 노동력 이외에는 팔 것이 없는 자유로운 임금노동자가 생겨나며, 생산자의 손을 떠난 생산수단을 자본으로 전환시키는 일이 가능하기 때문이다. 자본주의가 본격적으로 가동을 시작하려면, 그 전제조건으로 토지나 자본 혹은 노동력이 확보되어야만 하는 것은 하나의 상식이다. 이러한 본원적 축적이 이루어지는 과정에는 필연적으로 수탈과 불법, 폭력의 원리가 개입할 수밖에 없고, 한설야의 「과도기」는 식민지 조선에서 일어난 본원적 축적의 과정을 경향적인 시각에서 재현하는 데 성공한 작품이다.

「과도기」는 섣부른 관념으로 초월하거나 자연주의적 묘사에 매몰되지 않고, 창선이라는 민중이 느끼는 구체적 실감을 바탕으로 식민지 자본주의의 형성과정과 그것이 드리운 그늘을 형상화하는 데 성공하고 있다. 이것은 한국 현대소설사에서 매우 의미 있는 업적이라고 할 수 있다. 「과도기」는 이전의 신경향파 소설들이 생경한 이념만을 표백하거나 표피적 빈궁상에만 천착한 두 가지 경향을 변증법적으로 극복하고 있기 때문이다. 이것은 한설야가 식민지 조선의 산업화가 지닌 여러 문제점을 구체적인 현실 속에서 비판적으로 사유한 결과라

ment. Marx argued that capitalist development pre-supposes the separation of producers (farmers and craftsmen) from their means of production (land). It was in this way that the new free laborer class only had their labor power to sell and the capitalist class claimed the means of production freed from its producers. In order for capitalism to function fully, there necessarily needs to be land, capital, and a functioning labor force. This process of primitive accumulation is inevitably accompanied by princi-ples of exploitation, violence, and illegality. Han's "Transition" successfully and tendentiously repre-sent this process in colonial Chosun.

"Transition" succeeds in realistically depicting co-lonial capitalist formation and its shadowy under-belly from the perspective of Chang-seon, a con-crete character. Han brilliantly chooses to do this rather than merely follow formulaic ideas or bury itself in naturalistic details. This is significant work, then, as it dialectically overcomes two narrow ten-dencies of the Singyeonghyang School of the pre-ceding era—exposing crude ideas or presenting superficial descriptions of an abject reality. This is the result of Han's critical and concrete examina-tion of the problems accompanying colonial Cho-

고 할 수 있다.

그럼에도 이 작품에서 근대화되어 가는 현실에 대한 부정적인 시선만을 읽을 수 있는 것은 아니다. 그것은 창선이를 중심으로 한 서사 전개의 차원에서 발견할 수 있다. 「과도기」는 "창선이는 사 년 만에 옛땅으로 도라왔다"로 시작하여 "창선이는 요행 공장로동자로 쌥혓다. 상투 짜고 감발 치고 부삽 들고 콩크리-트 반죽하는 생소한 사람이 되엿다"로 끝난다. 창선은 결국 이 작품에서 비판적으로 묘사된 자본주의적 근대화의 물결에 동참하는 것이다. 이것은 고향 마을에 불어닥친 새로운 변화가 하나의 거대한 시대적 흐름임을 인정한 결과라고 볼 수도 있다. 한설야는 이러한 근대적 노동이 필연적으로 수반하는 생산관계의 문제점을 충분히 인식하고 있으면서도, 그러한 변화의 필연성만은 부정하지 못했던 것으로 판단된다.

sun industrialization.

Nevertheless, this story does not describe modernizing reality entirely negatively. Its narrative focus on Chang-seon begins with the lines "Chang-seon returned to his homeland after four years" and ends with "Luckily, Chang-seon was selected as a factory worker. He had his topknot cut, wrapped his feet with bandages, and became that strange man who would now take a shovel and knead the concrete." In other words, Chang-seon becomes, in the end, yet another participant of the capitalization critically described in this story. And we can interpret this as evidence that the author acknowledges this grand change as something irrevocable and thus, necessarily acceptable. Although Han Seol-ya was aware of the many problems associated with modern labor and productive relations, he could not deny its inevitability.

비평의 목소리

Critical Acclaim

이 시기에 에폭을 지은 작품은 역시 한설야의 「과도기」다. 이 작품은 현실에서 분열된 관념과 관념에서 떨어진 묘사의 세계를 단일한 메커니즘 가운데 형성하려고 한 최초의 작품이다. 그것을 가능케 한 것은 신경향파 시대와 근본에서는 같으나 그러나 그것보다는 일층 명백한 경향적인 정신이다. 그러므로 「과도기」는 그 양식에 있어서만 아니라 실로 그 정신에 있어서도 분명히 새 시대의 문학이다.

임화, 「소설문학의 20년」, 동아일보, 1940년 4월 20일.

「보복」에서 주인공의 행동은 오직 실패의 연속이었

Han Seol-ya's "Transition" is an epoch-establish-
ing work. It was Korean literature's first attempt to
overcome both concept dissociated from reality
and reality dissociated from concept, ultimately
combining both. This was possible because of his
indomitable spirit, clearly more tendentious than
the Sin'gyeonghyangpa's (New Tendentious School).
Thus, "Transition" is literature of a new age not
only in style but also in spirit.

Lim Hwa, "Twenty Years of Fiction," *Donga Ilbo*, 1940.

The protagonist in "Revenge" continues to expe-
rience one failure after another. But—how he

다. 그러나 실로 구하여 얻지 못하는 참상(慘傷)된 정열을 안고 마침내 반무의식 상태에서 무모의 세계에로 달리는 주인공의 몸부림! 거기에는 구제받기 이전의 비극! 그러나 동시에 체념하기 이전의 생명의 맥진이 있지는 않았을까. 그러나 그는 갱생의 노래에 의해서가 아니라 오직 광상곡에 의해서 반주되어지는 그러한 생명의 맥진이 있을 뿐이다. 따라서 우리는 여기에서 참상된 정열의 몸부림을 보며 지향(志向)하는 정열의 호곡을 듣는다.

안함광, 「지향하는 정열의 호곡」, 『동아일보』, 1939년 10월 7일~15일

「과도기」에 이르러 한국문학은 자본주의의 바깥으로 문학적 상상력이 나아갈 수 있는 길을 얻은 것이라고 할 수 있다. 「과도기」는 조선의 자본주의를 즉물적이고 즉자적으로 본 것도 아니고, 심정적 비판 차원에 머문 것도 아니며, 섣부른 관념으로 재단해 버린 것도 아니다. 「과도기」는 창선이라는 귀향자와 '창리' 마을을 내세워 조선 자본주의의 실상을, 그들이 약속하는 달콤한 미래의 허구성을 한편에서는 그 안으로부터, 다른 한편에서는 그 밖으로부터 묘파해낸 것이다. 이로써 우리는

struggles and charges semi-unconsciously into the reckless world, his passion disastrously wounded from these frustrations! In Han's work we can see tragedy before redemption! But at the same time in his work we can see the throbbing of life before resignation! But he has only the throbbing of life, accompanied not by a song of rebirth but by a rhapsody. Thus, we see here the passionate struggle of the wounded and the passionate wailing of the aspiring.

Ahn Ham-gwang, "Future-Oriented Passionate Lamentation," *Donga Ilbo*, 1939.

Korean literature has found a way for its imagination to go outside of capitalism only with the arrival of "Transition." This short story does not regard capitalism as something natural. Nor does it criticize it sentimentally or condemn it idealistically. "Transition" presents us with an incisive description of the capitalist reality in Chosun through the perspective of returned exile Chang-seon and through his hometown of Chang-ri. It criticizes the capitalist promise of a rosy future both internally and externally. Thus, in "Transition" we have an example of a literary critique of the capitalist social restruc-

「과도기」에서 식민지의 자본주의적 재편과정에 대한 문학적 비판의 한 사례를 얻게 된 것이다.

이현식, 「〈과도기〉 다시 읽기」,

『한설야 문학의 재인식』, 소명출판, 74쪽.

한설야는 해방 후 식민주의의 극복을 이전의 자신의 모습에 대한 비판으로 시작하였다. 민족이라고 하면 곧바로 민족주의를 연상하고 나아가 이는 계급운동 등을 반대하는 것으로만 생각하였던 이전의 계급환원주의를 비판함으로써 구각을 탈피하였고 진정한 식민주의의 극복의 길에 나섰던 것이다. 그리하여 계급환원론적 시각에 사로잡혀 있을 때 볼 수 없었던 많은 것들을 볼 수 있게 되었던 것이다. 이러한 점은 주변의 정황에 따른 정도와 밀도의 차이에도 불구하고 해방 후부터 1962년 숙청까지 지속적으로 이루어졌고 이론적으로 심화 확대되었다.

김재용, 「냉전적 분단구조하 한설야 문학의 민족의식과 비타협성」,

『분단구조와 북한문학』, 소명출판, 2000, 128쪽.

turing process during the colonial period.

Lee Hyeon-sik, "Re-reading 'Transition'," *A New Under-standing of Han Solya Literature* (Seoul: Somyong, 2000)

Han Seol-ya began his efforts to overcome colonialism after the liberation of Korea by criticizing his own actions during this period. He began by criticizing his previous heavily class-oriented attitude, a stance from which he'd regarded any attention to the nation as nationalism and criticized any opposing attitude as part of an opposing class movement. Thus, he was able to open his mind far more than when he'd reduced everything into matters of class. This new attitude of his continued to varying degrees until 1962, when he was eventually purged.

Kim Jae-yong, "National Consciousness and Uncompromising Will in Han Solya Literature Under the Cold War Division System," (Seoul: Somyong, 2000)

한설야

1900년 함경남도 함흥에서 이제마의 문하생인 아버지 한직연의 아들로 태어났다. 한직연은 토착 지주로서 군수를 지냈으며 이후에는 광산을 경영하기도 하였다. 1906년 함흥공립보통학교에 입학하였고, 1915년 경성제일고등보통학교에 입학하여 박헌영 등과 친교를 맺었으나 서울에 있는 서모와의 갈등 등으로 1918년 함흥고보로 전학하였다. 1919년 함흥법전에 진학하였으나 동맹휴교 사건에 연루되어 제적당하고 1920년부터 1년 남짓 북경 익지영어학교에서 사회과학을 수학하였다. 1921년 귀국 후 북청 학습강습소에서 교원 생활을 하였고, 이후 일본대학 사회학과로 유학을 갔다. 1923년 관동대지진으로 귀국하였고, 1925년 이광수의 추천으로 《조선문단》에 「그날 밤」을 발표하며 등단하였다. 1927년에 카프(KAPF)에 가입하여 계급문학의 옹호자로서 맹렬하게 활동한다. 이후 《신계단》, 《대조》, 《조선지광》의 편집에 관여하였고, 조선일보사 기자로도 활동하였다. 1934년에는 신건설사 사건으로 투옥된다. 1935년에

Han Seol-ya

Han Seol-ya was born in Hamheung, Ham-gyeongnam-do in 1900. His father, Han Jig-yeon, a landlord and Yi Je-ma's disciple, served as a *gun*-magistrate and managed a mine. Han Seol-ya entered Hamheung Public Elementary School in 1906 and entered Gyeongseong High School (Jeil Go-deung Botong Hakgyo) in Seoul in 1915, where he became friends with future social leaders like Pak Heon-yeong. He transferred to Hamheung High School in 1918 due to a personal conflict with his father's concubine in Seoul. He entered Hamheung Law School in 1919 but was expelled due to his involvement in a student strike. He then went to Beijing and studied social sciences at Ikchi English School for about a year. He returned home in 1921 and taught at Bukcheong Institute and then to Japan to study sociology at Japan University. In 1923, he returned home after the Great Kanto Earthquake.

He made his literary debut in 1925 when "That Night" was published in the *Chosun Mundan* upon Yi

집행유예로 석방되어 함흥으로 귀향하였고 인쇄소를 운영하였다. 1943년 유언비어 유포 혐의로 투옥되었고, 1944년 병보석으로 풀려난다. 1946년 북조선예술총동맹 결성에 핵심적인 역할을 수행하였으며, 북한 문인 중에 가장 먼저 김일성 형상화에 착수하였다. 해방 이후 북한문학의 건설에 핵심적인 역할을 수행하였으며, 최고인민회의 대의원, 조선문학예술총동맹 위원장, 교육상, 교육문화상 등의 핵심적인 지위를 계속 유지하였다. 1962년 종파주의자, 복고주의자, 일제시대 군수의 아들, 부와 방탕 등의 이유로 숙청당한 후, 1963년 자강도의 한 협동농장으로 보내진 것으로 알려져 있다.

Gwang-su's recommendation. He joined KAPF in 1927 and worked enthusiastically as an advocate of "class literature." He has since worked as editor for magazines like *Sin'gyedan, Daejo*, and *Chosunjigwang* as well as a reporter for the *Chosun Ilbo* newspaper. He was imprisoned for his activities related to KAPF in 1934 and was released in 1935. He returned home to Hamheung and managed a print shop. In 1943, he was imprisoned again for rumor mongering and released on bail due to illness in 1944.

Additionally, he played a central role in establishing the North Korean Artists Association in 1946. He began to craft a narrative describing Kim Il-sung for the first time in Korea. Also, he played an essential role in the establishment of North Korean literature and maintained leadership positions as the Supreme People's Assembly member, the president of the North Korean Artists Association, as well as its Minister of Culture and Minister of Culture and Education. In 1962 he was expelled from the all his positions upon accusations of being a sectarianist, a reactionary, the son of a *gun*-magistrate during the Japanese colonial period, as well as generally greedy and profligate. Upon expulsion he was sent to a collective in Jagang-do.

번역 **전승희** Translated by Jeon Seung-hee

서울대학교와 하버드대학교에서 영문학과 비교문학으로 박사 학위를 받았으며, 현재 하버드대학교 한국학 연구소의 연구원으로 재직하며 아시아 문예 계간지 《ASIA》 편집위원으로 활동 중이다. 현대 한국문학 및 세계문학을 다룬 논문을 다수 발표했으며, 바흐친의 『장편소설과 민중언어』, 제인 오스틴의 『오만과 편견』 등을 공역했다. 1988년 한국여성연구소의 창립과 《여성과 사회》의 창간에 참여했고, 2002년부터 보스턴 지역 피학대 여성을 위한 단체인 '트랜지션하우스' 운영에 참여해 왔다. 2006년 하버드대학교 한국학 연구소에서 '한국 현대사와 기억'을 주제로 한 워크숍을 주관했다.

Jeon Seung-hee is a member of the Editorial Board of *ASIA*, is a Fellow at the Korea Institute, Harvard University. She received a Ph.D. in English Literature from Seoul National University and a Ph.D. in Comparative Literature from Harvard University. She has presented and published numerous papers on modern Korean and world literature. She is also a co-translator of Mikhail Bakhtin's *Novel and the People's Culture* and Jane Austen's *Pride and Prejudice*. She is a founding member of the Korean Women's Studies Institute and of the biannual Women's Studies' journal *Women and Society* (1988), and she has been working at 'Transition House,' the first and oldest shelter for battered women in New England. She organized a workshop entitled "The Politics of Memory in Modern Korea" at the Korea Institute, Harvard University, in 2006. She also served as an advising committee member for the Asia-Africa Literature Festival in 2007 and for the POSCO Asian Literature Forum in 2008.

감수 **데이비드 윌리엄 홍** Edited by David William Hong

미국 일리노이주 시카고에서 태어났다. 일리노이대학교에서 영문학을, 뉴욕대학교에서 영어교육을 공부했다. 지난 2년간 서울에 거주하면서 처음으로 한국인과 아시아계 미국인 문학에 깊이 몰두할 기회를 가졌다. 현재 뉴욕에서 거주하며 강의와 저술 활동을 한다.

David William Hong was born in 1986 in Chicago, Illinois. He studied English Literature at the University of Illinois and English Education at New York University. For the past two years, he lived in Seoul, South Korea, where he was able to immerse himself in Korean and Asian-American literature for the first time. Currently, he lives in New York City, teaching and writing.

바이링궐 에디션 한국 대표 소설 089
과도기

2014년 11월 14일 초판 1쇄 발행

지은이 한설야 | 옮긴이 전승희 | 펴낸이 김재범
감수 데이비드 윌리엄 홍 | 기획위원 정은경, 전성태, 이경재
편집 정수인, 이은혜, 김형욱, 윤단비 | 관리 박신영 | 디자인 이준희
펴낸곳 (주)아시아 | 출판등록 2006년 1월 27일 제406-2006-000004호
주소 서울특별시 동작구 서달로 161-1(흑석동 100-16)
전화 02.821.5055 | 팩스 02.821.5057 | 홈페이지 www.bookasia.org
ISBN 979-11-5662-049-5 (set) | 979-11-5662-063-1 (04810)
값은 뒤표지에 있습니다.

Bi-lingual Edition Modern Korean Literature 089
Transition

Written by Han Seol-ya | **Translated by** Jeon Seung-hee
Published by Asia Publishers | 161-1, Seodal-ro, Dongjak-gu, Seoul, Korea
Homepage Address www.bookasia.org | **Tel**. (822).821.5055 | **Fax**. (822).821.5057
First published in Korea by Asia Publishers 2014
ISBN 979-11-5662-049-5 (set) | 979-11-5662-063-1 (04810)

금기와 욕망 Taboo and Desire